NEW
BABY

For Eli, the new baby - VB

For Jordan and Olivia - DA

First published in 2000 by Macmillan Children's Books
A division of Macmillan Publishers Limited
25 Eccleston Place, London SW1W 9NF
Basingstoke and Oxford
Associated companies throughout the world
www.panmacmillan.com

ISBN 0 333 76631 8 HB
ISBN 0 333 76632 6 PB

Text copyright © 2000 Valerie Bloom
Illustrations copyright © 2000 David Axtell
Moral rights asserted

1 3 5 7 9 8 6 4 2

A CIP catalogue record for this book is available from the British Library.

Printed in Belgium by Proost.

NEW
BABY

Written by Valerie Bloom

Illustrated by David Axtell

MACMILLAN
CHILDREN'S BOOKS

Me baby sister come home last week

Mama put her on the bed,

Then she pull back the little blanket

And I see the baby head.

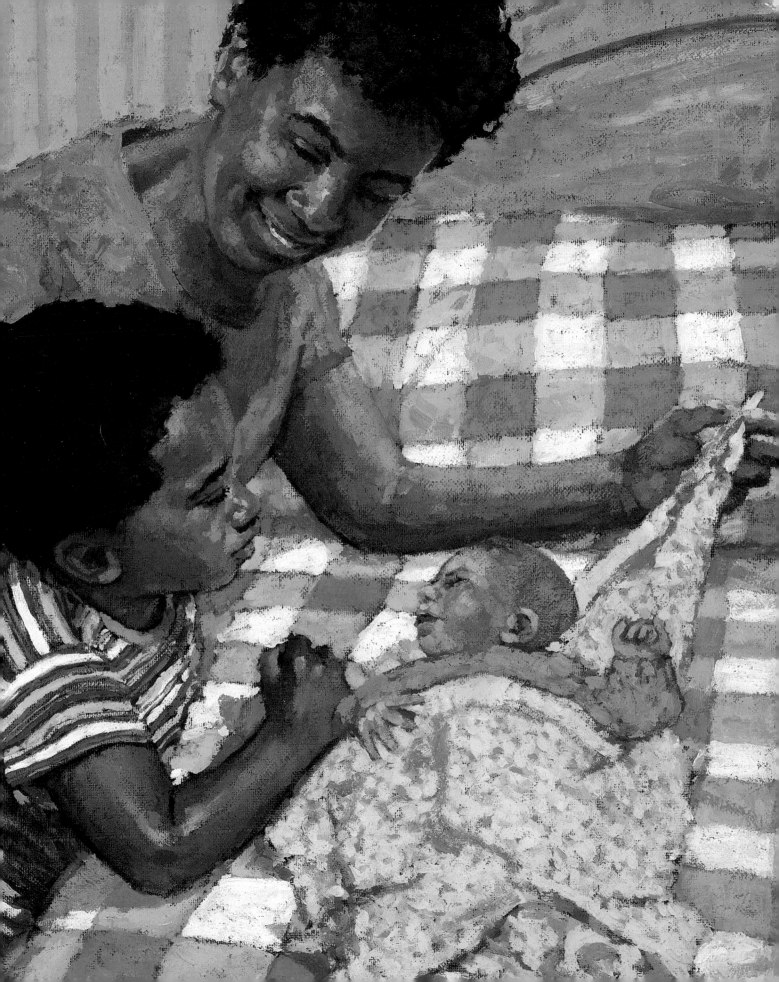

Two little bit a hair she have pon it,

And the little baby face

Wrinkle like she did fold up too tight

Inside Mama suitcase.

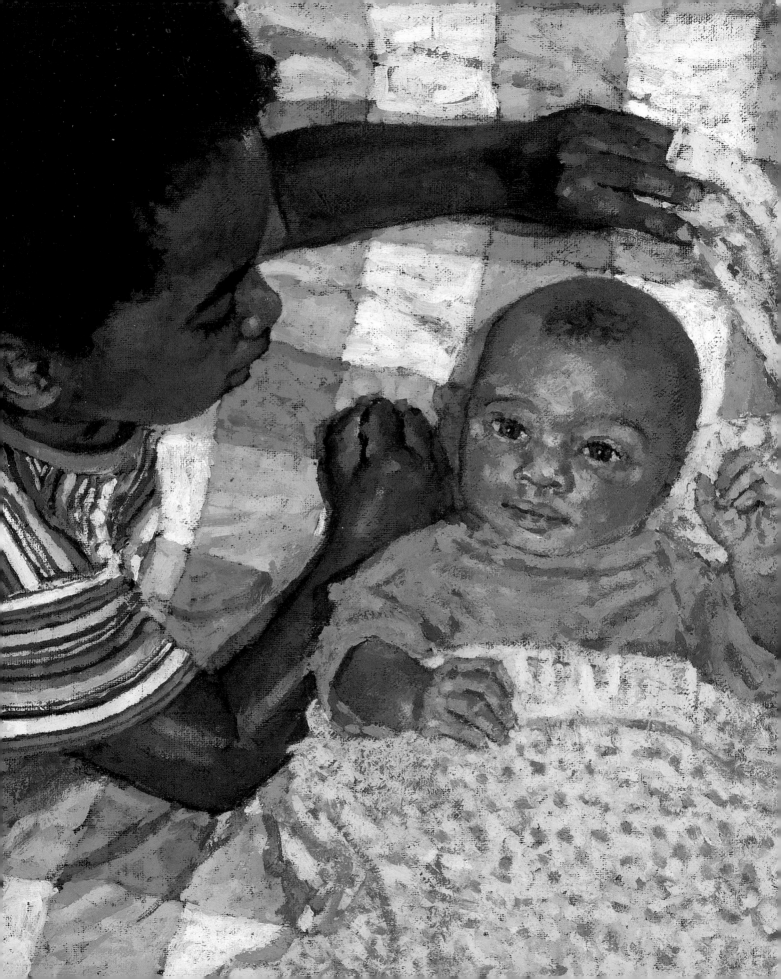

Mama say the baby hungry

So I give her piece a meat,

But Daddy say she can't eat yet

For she don't have no teeth.

I tell Mama to put her down

And let her play with me blue van,

Mama say the baby can't sit up yet

Nor hold things in her hand.

I say, "All right, maybe she would like

To play 'I Spy' with me."

They tell me baby can't talk yet,

An' she can hardly see.

All day long she eat and sleep,

She is a real ole sleepyhead,

But when night come, that little child

Will never settle in her bed!

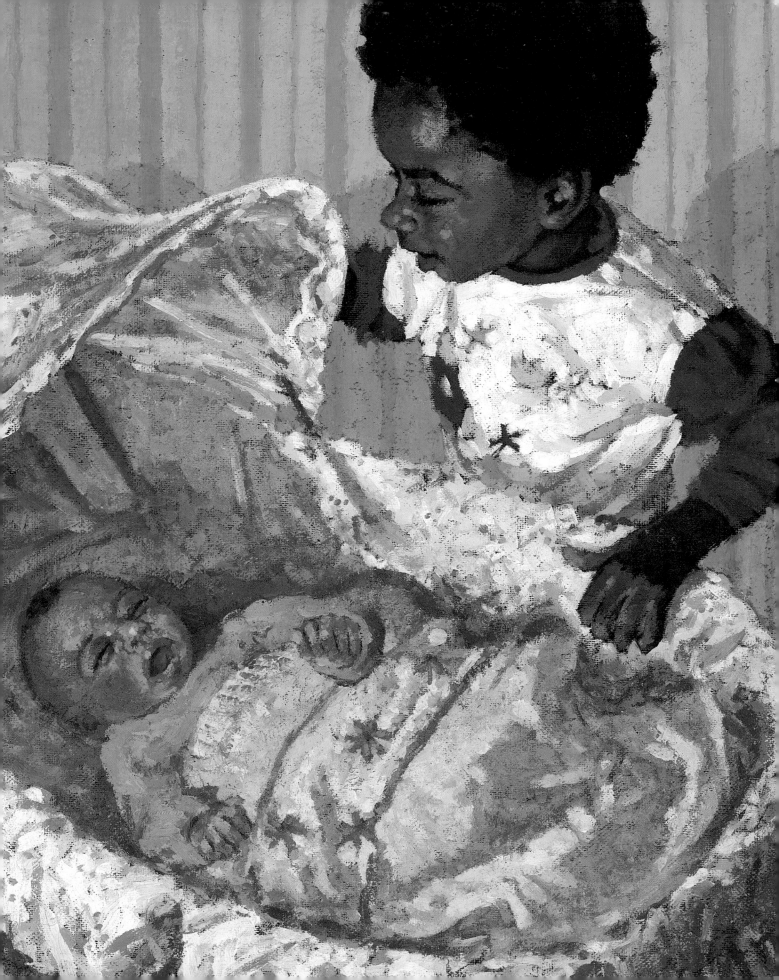

Her cryin' wake me every night,

I can hardly get any rest,

And as she wake she find the milk bottle

Mama have hide inside her chest.

Then Grandad and Nana come round,

If you hear them carry on!

"I never see such a pretty baby

From the day that ah was born."

I look pon Grandad and Nana,

I look good pon the baby,

I wonder if them was looking

At a different child from me.

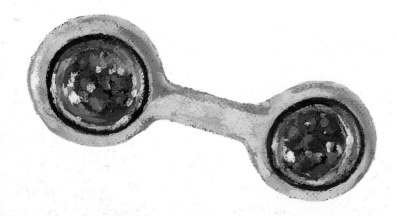

She ugly, she smelly, she stupid, she bald,

She can't walk or jump or run,

I wish Mama would take her back

And buy a different one.

Then Daddy plonk her in me lap!

"You want to hold her, Jay?"

I look pon him, I look pon her,

I was going to say, "No way!"

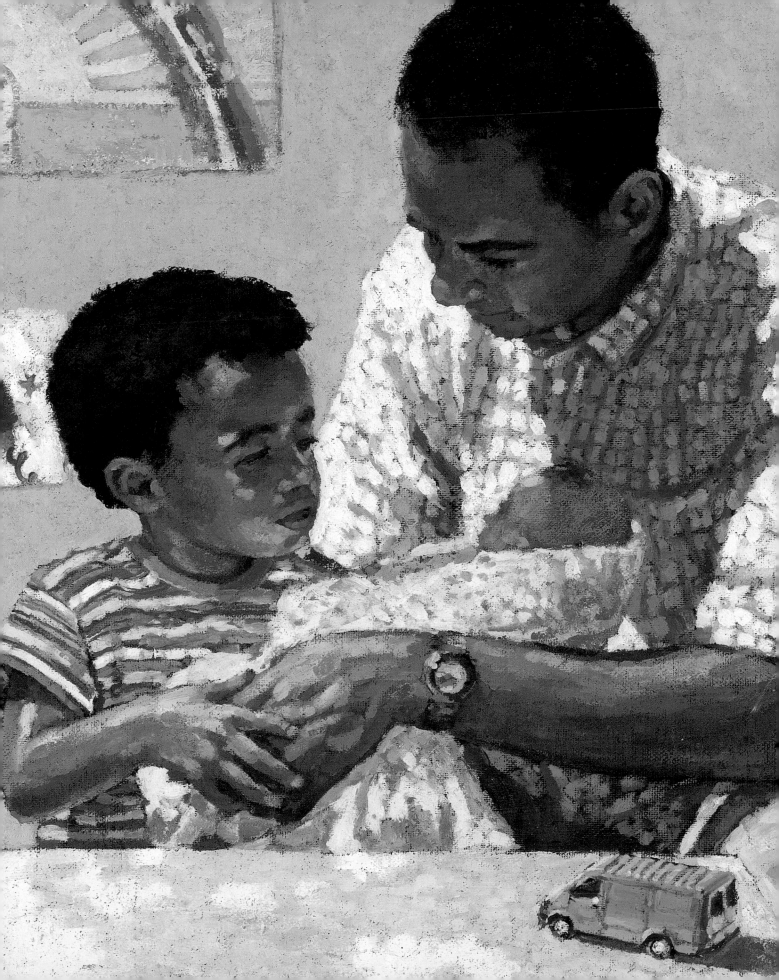

But then I look pon her crease-up face,

The little baby smile,

And I start to think that maybe

She not such an ugly child.

And then she start to laugh with me,

She hold me finger tight,

Dad say, "You know, Jay, I think

  she like you!"

Guess what? I think him right!

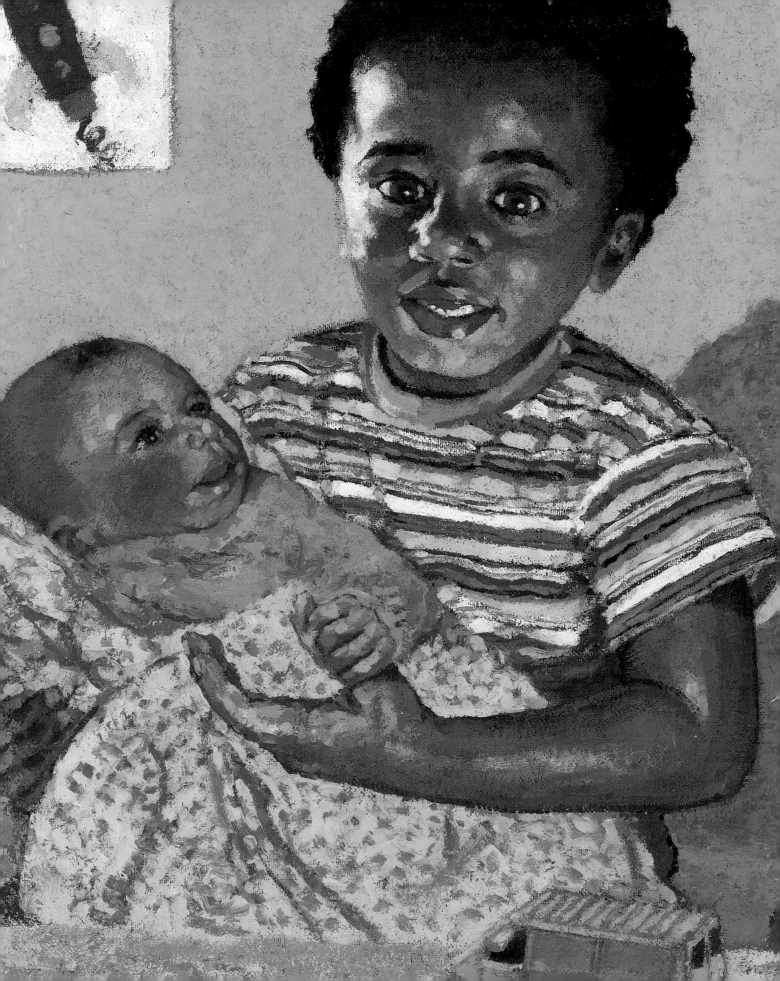

Valerie Bloom and David Axtell
are the author and illustrator of FRUITS,
winner of the Smarties Bronze Award.

MACMILLAN CHILDREN'S BOOKS